The A,B,Cs of Birding

written by Mariah Lee
photos by Mariah Lee
graphic designs by Mariah Lee

AuthorHouse™
1663 Liberty Drive
Bloomington, IN 47403
www.authorhouse.com
Phone: 1 (800) 839-8640

Because of the dynamic nature of the Internet, any web addresses or links contained in
this book may have changed since publication and may no longer be valid. The views
expressed in this work are solely those of the author and do not necessarily reflect the views
of the publisher, and the publisher hereby disclaims any responsibility for them.

Any people depicted in stock imagery provided by Getty Images are models,
and such images are being used for illustrative purposes only.
Certain stock imagery © Getty Images.

This book is printed on acid-free paper.

ISBN: 978-1-7283-3693-0 (sc)
ISBN: 978-1-7283-3694-7 (e)

Print information available on the last page.

Published by AuthorHouse 11/21/2019

authorHOUSE®

For Emma Faith

To the BIG people
(sharing this book with smaller people),

I hope you will enjoy learning about
 birds as much as I do. I am not an
expert. Fifteen years ago I moved to
Galveston, Texas. I saw so many birds
I had never seen living in New England.

I bought a field guide, a notebook, and
a cheap camera. Beautiful birds were all
around and I was excited to learn about them.
I eventually got a digital camera. I am not a
professional photograper but the photos in this
book were all taken by me.

WARNING:
GollyGee asks a lot of questions! It's okay
to NOT know all of the answers. How
powerful for your child to see that you
are still learning also.

There is a box on every page where i have
shared something that has made my bird
watching and bird photography more rewarding.

My hope is that this book inspires you!
Enjoy!!!

a,b,c,d,e,f,g
Hi. My name is GollyGee

h and i and j and k
We can look at birds today!

l,m,n,o and p
Feathered friends just like me.

q and r and s and t
Some are big and some are wee.

u, v, w, x and y
Don't be shy. Ask WHAT and WHY!

and finally z!
Turn the page and fly with me ...

a is for avocet

Avocets have long legs.
Can you guess why?

Look at their beaks.
Do they curve up
or down?

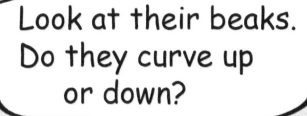

Avocets are shorebirds.

Avocets like to feed in flocks.
How many avocets do you see?

They all move together. Their bills
swoop left then right and catch
little sea bugs. Can you move your
arms like their bills?

Want to get a close up photo?
Take a picture where you are
then slowly & quietly step closer.
Take another picture. Repeat
until the bird flies away!

b is for bill

All **b**ills open and close like your mouth. This long **b**illed curlew has a decurved **b**ill. Can you guess where and how he looks for food?

This is a white pelican. What do they catch in their pouch bill?

It looks like this humming bird is drinking nectar with a straw but it is not!
It has a long bill that catches insects when it's flying. Hummers have long tongues that lap up the nectar from flowers.

Buy a bird guide.
Match your photo to
the picture in the book.

c is for cardinal

This is a MALE cardinal.
Boys, dads, & uncles are male.
What color is this male
cardinal?

Cardinals have a short,
thick, cracking beak.
What do you think
they eat?

The cardinal is the official
bird for seven states.
What is your state bird?

This is a FEMALE cardinal.
How does she look different from the male?
Do you see the tuft of feathers on their
heads? That is called a crest.

Do you like to sing? Cardinals can sing
28 different songs! A hatchling can sing
it's first song when it's only 3 weeks old.

Transfer your photos to your computer
after every outing. Your card
will have room to take new
pictures every time!

d is for duck

This is a mallard duck family.
The female is called a duck. She
is brown and grey and says "Quack".

The male is called a drake. He has a
bright green head and he says
"Breeeeze".

Most female ducks are brown and
dull. Can you guess why?

Mallard ducks are dabbling ducks. They eat plants and bugs on the surface of the water.

BUT, diving ducks (like scaups) are heavy and look for food deep under water.

Wear clothing colors that blend with the environment. (Think camouflage.)

e is for egret

This is a snowy egret.

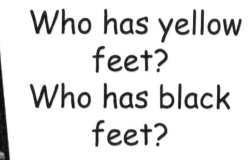

Who has yellow feet?
Who has black feet?

Who has a yellow bill?
Who has a black bill?

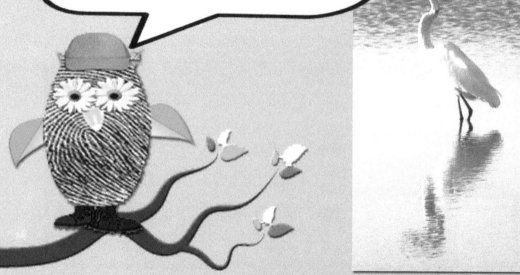

This is a great egret.

This is a cattle egret.

You will find her eating in fields following cows, horses or tractors that stir up frogs,grasshoppers and crickets.
Great egrets have long necks and are as tall as a three year old child! Snowy egrets are not as big. Who has the shortest neck?

Don't wait for the perfect shot. Shoot. Shoot. Shoot! Keep trying.

f is for flight

(Penguins and ostriches don't fly.)

All birds have wings and feathers. This hummingbird flaps it's wings 3,600 times per minute!

White pelicans are one of the heaviest flying bird. They can weigh as much as a car tire!

This white ibis has a recurved bill.

Who has yellow feet and a black bill?

Bug Repellent!
Spray your clothing!

g is for gull

There are 28 types of gulls in the USA. Many immature gulls have brown streaked plumage.

This gull says, "ha ha ha ha"! Can you guess it's name? (a laughing gull) ha ha ha ha!

Gulls have webbed feet and are strong swimmers. Who else has webbed feet?

This gull wants to sit on the pelican's head. She wants to be ready to steal food from the pelican's pouch! Thief!

Make friends with your ZOOM lens.

h is for hawk

All hawks have strong hooked bills, short necks and curved talons. They hunt mice, squirrels and snakes from a high perch on the edge of a field.

A red tailed hawk was sitting atop a pole that stood between the road and a large field. Can you guess why?

I had my zoom lens, but as soon as I picked up my camera the hawk flew two poles away. I followed and he flew back to the first pole! We did this everyday for a week!

The last day I saw this hawk, he flew down and sat on the fence post right across the street. I took one picture as he stared at me and another as he flew away!

Binoculars! Find a pair that's right for you!

i is for ibis

Ibis have long recurved bills. Sometimes they are orange.

But when ibis are looking to start a family their bills and legs turn bright red! This is called their breeding plumage.

When ibis fly you can see the black feathers on the tips of their wings.

Look carefully! These are not all ibis.

What egrets hang out with ibis?

Keep your lens clean with special wipes. Cover your lens when not in use.

j is for juvenile

This is a family of sandhill cranes.

The juvenile crane is the same size as his parents but somethings are different.What color is the juvenile sandhill crane's head?
The male and female cranes look alike. Did you notice the bright red feathers above their eyes?

k is for kingfisher

This is a male belted kingfisher. Female kingfishers have a bright chestnut chest band.

The largest kingfisher lives in Australia. The kookaburra! (Do you know that song?)

The belted kingfishers have a heavy bill,
a large head with a crest and white under parts.

You can find them sitting high on wires waiting
to dive into a creek, pond or marsh after fish,
large insects and lizards.

Can you imagine this!
The oldest known kingfisher fossil
was found in Florida.
It is 2 million years old!

Learn how to put your
photos on your computer.
You can make them large
there to see details!

l is for lore

The lore is the small area on each side of a bird's face. The area between it's eyes and the base of the upper part of it's bill.

These are both snowy egrets. Do you see his yellow feet and black bill? When he's looking for a mate his lore turns bright yellow.

What color is this common egret's lore? Their feathers change to wispy plumes when attracting a mate.

Who are the pink birds roosting with the egrets? Hint: They are not flamingos.

Stop. Listen. Look!

m is for migration

In the fall or winter, birds will migrate (move) from places in the North to areas in the South. They are looking for food and warmer weather.

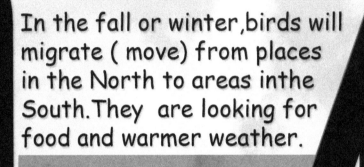

Hummingbirds will fly nonstop for 26 hours when they migrate across the Gulf of Mexico

Birds will migrate again in the spring. They will travel back to the North looking for the best place to build a nest that's near food.

There are day migrants like pelicans and hummers who can eat while they fly.

Scissortail flycatchers are night migrants. They need to rest and eat during the day.

Buy a bird guide.
Match your photos to the pictures in the book.

n is for nest

A nest is a bird's home. It can be on a roof, dug in the sand or made with twigs and leaves attached to tree branches. How many nests do you see?

This mama spoonbill feeds her 3 downy nestlings in the nest. In a month or so they will be called juveniles. They will be as big as an adult and have pale pink feathers for flying.

These great egrets found a mate and built a nest. Did you notice their green lores?

This egret is nestled atop her nest waiting for her eggs to hatch!

shhh ...
Whisper. Walk quietly.

o is for owl

This is my cousin the burrowing owl.

Most owls are awake and finding food during the night. BUT the burrowing owl hunts for lizzards, frogs and beetles during the day.

Most owls have a flat face, a circle of feathers around their eyes and a hawk-like beak.

Owl eyes are fixed in their heads so they have to turn their whole head to look left or right. Can you hold your head still and move just your eyes to see someone standing next to you? An owl can't!

Because owls have14 vertebrae in their necks (people have only 7!) they can turn their head almost all the way around! How far can you turn your head?

Owls have special feathers that don't make noise when they are flapped. This helps them sneak up on their dinner!

Organize your photos. Sort them into folders according to date, or place, or bird name.

p is for pelican

There are two kinds of pelicans. White pelicans and brown pelicans. How many brown pelicans are flying in this picture?

All pelicans have a pouched bill, short legs, webbed feet and a large body.

But brown pelicans don't hang out with white pelicans. White pelicans like inland lakes and brown pelicans like the southern and western seacoasts.

They all eat fish and need to eat about 4 pounds of fish every day!

Sunscreen!
Keep reapplying it.

q is for question

What makes a bird a bird?

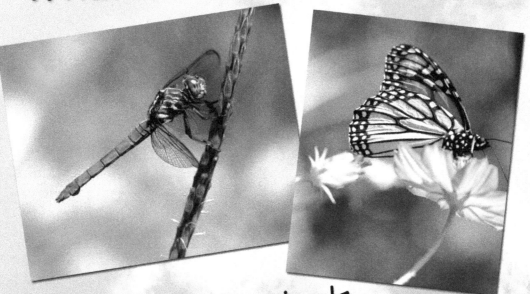

Are birds the only animals that have wings?

no!

Are birds the only animals with a bill or beak?

no!

Are birds the only animals that lay eggs?

no!

r is for rookery

A rookery is a collection of nests high in a clump of trees. These photos were taken at Smith Oaks Rookery in High Island, Texas.

s is for sandhill crane

Male and female sandhill cranes stay with their mates for 20 years or more!

The sandhill cranes have gathered in this field to eat roots, seeds and mice.

Adult sandhill cranes have a red crown and a pale cheek. Juveniles have brown head feathers. They will stay with their parents for almost a year.

Sandhill cranes have a distinctive rolling cry that can be heard for miles.

Photos of the landscape or seascape will give clues to ID the bird.

t is for tern

royal tern- adult

foster's tern- adult

foster's terns- juvenile

Royal terns lay only one egg in their nest.Both parents will take turns sitting on that egg for 30 days.

Foster's terns can lay 4 eggs in their nest. Both parents will feed the young while they are still in the nest.

Within a few days after hatching, a royal tern leaves the nest and joins a creche. Both parents bring it food. They feed only their own young that they recognize by voice.

Both royal terns and foster's terns are plunge divers. They hover over marshes, bays and beaches and dive just below the surface to catch fish. They also eat insects, frogs and crabs.

Who has an orange bill? Who has a black spot of feathers near their eyes?

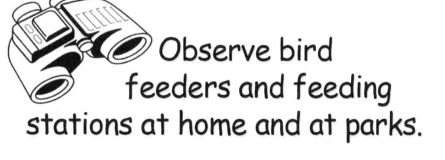

Observe bird feeders and feeding stations at home and at parks.

u is for unique

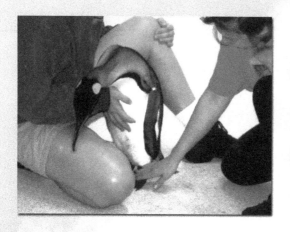

This is a king penguin.

Why are penguins unique birds?

~Because penguins don't fly! They do have feathers, tiny dense feathers that keep them warm. Most penguins live south of the equater where it's cold.

~Because penguins are great swimmers! Penguins have webbed feet and their wings have turned into flippers. Their body is the perfect shape to glide through water.

v is for vulture

These turkey vultures have light grey heads.

They are juvenile turkey vultures.

Vultures can only hiss and grunt. They have no syrinx, the organ that makes sounds.
Truth:
If someone bothers them, they throw up on them!!!!

Adult turkey vultures look like turkeys with their red featherless heads and short hooked ivory bills

Vultures can't kill their prey. They eat animals that are already dead. These dead animals give off a gas that only vultures can smell.

Vultures can soar for hours without flapping their wings. Pilots have seen them flying at 20,000 feet!

Bring a notebook and pen to write down questions & observations.

w is for willet

Willets are waders with a thick long bill. Male and female birds look the same. Willets have grey feathers on top. What color are their feathers below?

They feed in salt marshes and bays. A common shorebird, the willet eats fiddler crabs, small fishes and marine worms.

Pack extra batteries and fully charge your rechargeable ones.

x is for extraordinary

Hummingbirds are extraordinary!!!
They are like living helicopters!
They can hover, fly backwards,
shift sideways, and fly straight
up and down!

y is for yellow crowned night heron

Immature (we can also say juvenile) yellow crowned night herons don't have a yellow crown yet. Can you guess why they are streaked?

Adult yellow crowned night herons have a distinct black and white pattern on their face. They have a thick bill and a long thin neck.

Can you see this heron's yellow crown? The crown is the very top of the head.

There are two types of night herons. The other is a black crowned night heron. Can you guess what color the feathers are on the top of his head?

Bring your camera! Any photo will help you remember details.

z is for zoo

Gabe is a blue and gold macaw.
He lives in the forests in South
America and Central America.

In the USA, birds like Gabe and Cookie live in zoos. People have an opportunity to see birds that live in the wild in other countries.

Cookie is a yellow crested cockatoo all the way from Indonesia.

Bring a hat and sunglasses.

glossary

Australia A country south of the equator that is also an island that is home to many colorful birds.

bird guide (field guide) A book that has pictures and facts about birds in specific areas.

breeding plumage The layers of colorful feathers that cover some male birds typically in the spring when they are looking for a mate.

camouflage Many female and juvenile birds have feathers that are in colors to hide them in their environment.

creche A flock of unrelated young birds brought together for protection often guarded by one parent while the others rest or forage for food.

curlew A large wading bird with a long decurved bill.

decurved bill A bird's bill that turns downward.

equator The imaginary line that divides the globe in half.. The closer to the equator, the closer to the sun, and the hotter the weather.

Galveston, Texas An island on the Gulf of Mexico that is a popular spot to observe birds migrating.

hooked bill A strongly curved bill or jaw as in parrots and cockatoos.

iridescent Showing luminous colors that seem to change when seen from different angles.

kookaburra A brownish bird from Australia that is a type of kingfisher. Do you know the kookaburra song?

recurved bill A bill that curves upward like on a avocet.

shorebird A wading bird like a willet, sandpiper or plover that is found along shallow sandy beaches.

talons The large hooked claws (feet) on birds of prey like hawks and eagles.

vertebrae The small bones that make up the backbone.

waders Long legged birds like herons that are found along the shore and mudflats.

webbed feet (webbed toes) The fusion of 2 or more toes on ducks, frogs and kangaroos!

Aren't birds AMAZING! I'm so happy I got to spend 26 letters learning about them with you. Keep asking questions!

Lightning Source UK Ltd.
Milton Keynes UK
UKHW051912041219
354766UK00005B/93/P